GRUMPUS

BY MAUREEN PATCHING

ILLUSTRATED BY JANINE PATCHING

GRUMPUS

THE ADVENTURES OF A BEAR CUB

Matador
9 Priory Business Park,
Wistow Road, Kibworth Beauchamp,
Leicestershire. LE8 0RX
Tel: 0116 279 2299
Email: books@troubador.co.uk
Web: www.troubador.co.uk/matador
Twitter: @matadorbooks

ISBN 978 1789013 290

British Library Cataloguing in Publication Data.
A catalogue record for this book is available from the British Library.

Printed and Bound in the UK by 4Edge Limited
Typeset in 11pt Minion Pro by Troubador Publishing Ltd, Leicester, UK

Matador is an imprint of Troubador Publishing Ltd

Created for Dylan Patching

Contents

GRUMPUS PLAYS A TRICK ON HIS FRIENDS

Our story is about a brown furry bear cub, who has big brown eyes, a brown nose and a very fat body. His name is Grumpus, he is called this because he has such a grumpy looking face, in fact, he is a very happy bear who loves playing with his friends. He also loves eating and will eat anything he can when his mother isn't looking.

'Mother, can I go and play with Spike and Ted?'

Spike and Ted were brothers and were Grumpus's best friends.

'You can go, but make sure you are back for tea,' said Mother.

So Grumpus went off down the path to find his friends and, after a short while, he saw them play-fighting by the little pond.

I'll give them a surprise and play a trick on them,

he thought. So, he climbed up a very old tree that had lots of dark green leaves on its big branches and he started to whistle and chirrup like a bird – 'chirrup, chirrup, tweet, tweet.'

'Can you hear that noise?' asked Spike. 'I wonder what it is?'

'Sounds like a bird of some sort,' replied Ted, 'but I've never heard that one before, have you?'

'No, I haven't.'

'It seems to be coming from that tree on the other side of the lake. Let's go around and see if we can see it.'

So, the pair of them went over to the gnarled old tree, stood quietly at its base and looked up.

'I can't see anything, can you?'

'No, and I can't hear anything now either.'

Grumpus was by this time, enjoying himself and was laughing so much that he didn't notice the branch on which he was clinging was beginning to creak and groan under his weight.

'Shall we climb up the tree to get a closer look?' asked Spike.

'If you want,' said timid Ted nervously, 'but you had better go up first as you are smaller and much quicker than me.'

'Okay.'

Spike, who was called Spike because he had a spiky tuft of fur between his ears, didn't argue, but climbed swiftly up the old trunk and crawled along the creaking branch from where the strange bird noise had come. He nearly toppled onto the ground again when he saw Grumpus sitting at the end of the branch just laughing.

'What are you doing?' whispered Spike. 'Did you hear that strange bird too?'

But before Grumpus had time to answer, Ted, who had followed closely behind Spike, was now edging along the branch to where the other two were sitting, and just as he was about to ask Grumpus the same question the tree gave one final groan, and with an enormous cracking noise the old branch snapped into pieces.

Crash, crunch.

'Ooh!' 'Ouch!' 'Oh!'

Splish, splash, splosh.

And they all landed in the lake.

'I can't swim,' yelled Spike.

'Neither can I,' shrieked Ted, but Grumpus was laughing again, sitting up to his waist in the shallow water.

'You don't need to swim,' shouted Grumpus, 'it's very shallow and if you stand up you'll see the water only comes up to your knees.'

First Spike and then Ted stood up. All three bears looked at one another then started to splash about and play tag in the water. They were having such fun they forgot the time, until it was quite late.

In the meantime, Mother had been very worried because a little earlier in the day she had seen some hunters with guns walking through the woods, so when she saw the little bears coming up the path, still playing and soaking wet, she was very relieved but also cross.

'Grumpus, come here immediately, get dry and then go straight to bed. There'll be no supper for you tonight.'

'But, Mother, I am so hungry,' cried Grumpus pulling such a long face he really did look very grumpy.

'Perhaps this will teach you to come home on time,' she said, looking stern.' Then, turning to the two brothers, she told them to go home immediately as their mother would be worried too and it would soon be dark.

So, with a wave to Grumpus, both Spike and Ted ran off down the path and into the forest as quickly as their little legs would carry them. They didn't like the forest in the dark and already the shadows of the trees were growing longer, and the sun was almost gone.

FORAGING

'Hello Mother,' said Grumpus. 'Sorry I came back late last night. Can I have some breakfast now, please?'

'Good morning, Grumpus. There are only a few nuts for breakfast this morning because today we are going to start your lessons on foraging. You're getting older and it's time you learnt how to get some of your own food.'

Grumpus looked startled. *Just some nuts? I'll fade away*, he thought.

The little bear looked very grumpy as he followed his mother into the woods, but he felt excited to be going out looking for food. He knew he could eat some berries so when he saw some lovely round shiny black ones on a bush near to the path, he couldn't resist picking one. His mother turned around just as he was putting it into his mouth. She didn't say a word, just waited.

'Oh, it's horrible,' cried Grumpus, and he spat it out onto the ground.

'Those berries are not good for us, they're for the birds,' said Mother. 'It's important for you to learn which nuts, roots and berries you can eat safely when you are in the woods. Sometimes, the berries look really tasty, but they can be very bitter and sometimes they can be poisonous and make you sick. So never eat anything until you know it's safe.

Now these black ones over here are lovely,' she said. 'They are blackberries and we can eat these, and the red ones over in the corner are very good for you, they are redcurrants. Go and try some of those.' Grumpus was very happy.

Eventually they came to a tree where Mother stopped, looked up into the branches and pointed to where some bees were very busy flying in and out of holes in the tree trunk.

'Grumpus, I am going to reach up there to get some honey. If you want some you'll have to climb up to where the holes are because you are too small to reach them from here.'

It was an easy climb for Grumpus. He went up the tree quickly until he reached the part of the trunk which had the holes and the buzzing bees.

Mother stretched up and pulled away a large piece of tree bark with her long claws then put her paw inside; she drew out a sticky piece of golden honeycomb. The bees were very cross and circled round her, but her fur was too thick for them to sting her.

'Your turn,' said Mother. 'Use your claws and break off a piece of bark, reach in and pull out a piece of honeycomb and then come down.'

Grumpus was very scared and was trembling but he clawed at the bark which came away easily and very carefully put his little paw inside; however, he couldn't reach the honeycomb. He stretched further, and still further until he couldn't stretch anymore, but still he couldn't reach. The bees were furious now and buzzed crossly all around him.

'Go away, go away. I don't want to hurt you, I just want a little of your honey,' shouted Grumpus. And with that he let go of the branch to wave them away and lost his balance.

Down, down and down he went, crashing through the leaves.

'Ouch! Ouch!' he cried.

And then, just before he hit the ground his mother held out her big paw and caught him.

'I didn't get any honey,' wailed Grumpus, 'and the bees were very cross, and I was frightened.'

'You'll learn, and it'll get easier as you get bigger. Don't cry, I have plenty for both of us.'

Later that day, Grumpus went down the path towards the little pond to meet Spike and Ted and to tell them about his morning of foraging and honey collecting.

'It was such fun,' he lied.

'I went foraging with our older brother Jon-Jon last week,' said Ted, 'but I didn't get any honey. I was too scared.'

'Oh, there's nothing to be scared about,' lied Grumpus again.

'I have never been honey collecting,' said Spike. 'Can you take us tomorrow, Grumpus?'

'Well. Err... um, I don't think I can

tomorrow. I shall be very busy. Sorry! Oh, I should get home now. Mustn't be late. See you soon. Bye.' And with that, Grumpus scampered as fast as he could back home.

SWIMMING LESSONS

The next day when Grumpus got up he could see his mother standing next to an enormous bear with huge muscles and great big paws. They were talking quietly about the hunters in the valley.

'Father,' shouted Grumpus, as he bounced excitedly over the grass and flung himself onto one of his father's big furry legs.

'Hello, little man,' he said, as he swung his son up onto his broad shoulders.

'At last you're awake! Your mother has been telling me about how she took you foraging in the woods for berries and honey yesterday. So now I think it's time you learnt to swim, so when you have finished breakfast we will go to the river.'

Grumpus had to walk very fast to keep up with his father's long strides and they soon reached the edge of the pond where

Grumpus usually met Spike and Ted. This morning they were playing there again.

'Oh, look, Father, my friends are here.'

'I'm going to learn to swim,' Grumpus shouted to them.

However, when the two brothers looked up and saw the huge brown bear walking behind Grumpus, they both hid behind a tree and didn't answer.

'Am I learning to swim here?' asked Grumpus happily.

'No, son, the water is too shallow here. We need to go to the river where it is much deeper.'

'Oh!' said Grumpus worriedly.

'You'll be fine. I wouldn't let anything happen to you.'

They walked on until they reached the chosen spot. The riverbank seemed very steep to Grumpus and he wondered how he would even manage get into the water.

'Right! Now I want you to climb up on my back and hang on tight.'

Up climbed Grumpus and put his paws firmly around his father's neck while they went into the river.

'As we get in deeper, I'll bend down, and you'll slide off. I'll keep your head up by holding onto the scruff of your neck and you'll paddle your legs as though you are running fast; this will keep you moving and stop you from sinking. It's called the doggy paddle stroke.'

They went nearer the middle until the water was up to his father's waist.

'Okay, off you go, slide down.'

Grumpus slid down into the water, paddling his little legs as fast as he could go. It was such hard work. But he was swimming! Well, almost! His father still held him by the neck, but he was swimming just the same.

'You're doing well, so I'm going to let go and I want you to swim on your own.'

'I don't think I am ready Fath—'

'Bubble, bubble, bubble.'

When Grumpus opened his mouth, he swallowed a big gulp of water, which made him forget all about paddling his legs and he started to sink. Father was there immediately, and with one big paw he pulled him to safety.

'Splutter, splutter, cough, cough. I didn't like that very much,' cried Grumpus.

'That was quite good, but you must keep your legs paddling and go slower, then you won't get so tired. But most importantly, remember to keep your mouth closed.'

Grumpus practised and practised, and by lunchtime he could swim all by himself. He was very happy, very wet, very hungry and so very tired that his father had to carry him home.

'You did well, but until you are bigger and more experienced I don't want you going swimming on your own as it can be dangerous. Do you understand?'

But Grumpus didn't hear anything, he was curled up fast asleep on the floor. He hadn't even eaten his lunch.

FISHING

Spike, Ted and Grumpus were playing hide and seek in the woods when it started to rain, and rain very hard. Big drops of water came splashing down on their heads from the wet leaves above them and huge puddles were forming.

'Oh! What are we going to do now, guys?' asked Grumpus. 'I don't want to go home yet, do you?'

'No,' the two brothers replied in unison.

'Well if we're going to get wet, we might as well get very wet and go over to the big lake over the hill and try and catch us some fish,' said Spike, whose once spikey fur looked a bit flat and soggy.

'We're not supposed to go that far,' Ted whispered, but the other two ignored him.

'It's a great idea,' said Grumpus, who was always hungry and loved fish.

Do you know how to catch fish, Spike?' asked Grumpus.

'Well, not really, but we did see our brother Jon-Jon catch some the other day and it seemed easy enough. You wade into the water, you keep very still, then, when a fish swims near, you pounce on it and grab it in your mouth.'

'Sounds good. Let's go and catch us some fish then.'

They reached the lake and walked into the water up to their knees. They kept very still, but as more rain fell the water became deeper and the bears started to wobble, which made them wobble even more. So, they didn't see a big fish swim towards them until it had jumped out of the water, swished its large silvery tail from side to side, fall back into the water and swim slowly away. Unfortunately, his swishing tail had caught Grumpus hard on his nose.

'Ouch, that really hurt!' cried Grumpus, and he went to sit on the bank with his eyes watering and his nose red and throbbing.

Meanwhile, Spike thought he saw a little

fish hiding in the reeds. So, with all his strength, he pounced, only to find it was a rough piece of wood.

'Ouch!' he cried, as a big splinter of wood went into his big toe. 'That really hurt!' He hobbled slowly to the bank and sat next to Grumpus, whose nose was very red, and his eyes were still watering.

Seeing the other two in trouble, Ted thought it might be safer for him to look for fish by the water's edge where it was shallower, but as he poked amongst the reeds, a sleeping water rat, who didn't like being disturbed, nipped Ted's paw with his sharp teeth. 'Ouch, that hurt!' wailed Ted. And when he saw the rat was about to nip him again he quickly jumped out of the water and sat next to his companions. 'I think I prefer picking berries and digging for roots,' said Ted, rubbing his sore paw. 'It's safer.'

'I don't like fishing much either,' agreed Grumpus, with his bright red nose.

'Neither do I,' whispered Spike, as he tried to remove the splinter from his big toe. 'But what shall we do now?'

'I know, there's a big yellow ball over there under that little tree. Let's play catchers,' suggested Grumpus.

'Good idea, give it to me first,' shouted Spike.

'No, to me!' shrieked Ted.

But before Grumpus had even reached the ball, there were four loud bangs. Bang! Bang! Bang! Bang! The bears froze.

'Are they gunshots?' asked Spike.

'I believe so,' said Ted timidly, 'we should go, it could be the hunters your mother saw the other day and we're not supposed to be so far from home and I feel quite frightened.'

'They sound a long way away, but I'll come with you,' said Grumpus.

As the gang of three cubs walked up the hill homeward, they heard more shots ring out across the valley, but they didn't see a man hiding in the bushes.

It was then that Grumpus remembered they had left the football down by the brambles.

'I'm going to get our ball. You two go ahead and I'll catch you up.'

He soon found it, but as he bent to pick it up he heard a muffled cry and then a yelping sound. He waited and listened and then he heard it again – it was coming from deep amongst the bushes.

DOG

'Hello,' he called. 'Is anyone there?'

'Oh, help me, please. I'm caught up in these brambles and I cannot move.'

Grumpus peered in and saw a small bundle of brown fur, which looked like a young bear cub.

'Hold on, I'm coming,' he said, and quickly pulled the prickly brambles away until he had reached the little brown bundle.

'Oh, you're a strange little bear if ever I saw one, and you have a long tail!'

'Oh, please don't hurt me.'

'I won't hurt you, I'm rescuing you, but you don't look much like a bear.'

'That's because I'm a dog,' said the little dog indignantly.

'You look very young, what are doing in the woods all by yourself?'

'I was sold to one of the hunters from the

town. He was kind to me, but when he and his friends started shooting I became afraid and ran away. I then became entangled in these bushes.'

'What's your name?'

'Dog is what my first master called me,

but his son Dylan called me his Little Dog and my mother was called Old Dog.'

'Please to meet you, Little Dog. I'm Grumpus, I shall call you Dog.'

'Why are you called Grumpus? It's a strange name.'

'Because my mother thought I had grumpy face when I was born, but I'm not a grumpy bear. I'm a happy one. However, I had better hurry home in case those hunters come near here. You seem very frightened. Would you like to come home with me?'

'Oh yes please. I would like that, I don't want to be a hunting dog. I used to like living on the farm with Dylan and all the farm animals.'

'Come on then, we'd better hurry.'

Grumpus looked out for Ted and Spike on the way back, but they had already disappeared into the woods and he couldn't see or hear them.

'And what have we here?' asked Mother, looking down at the trembling puppy.

But before Grumpus could answer, Father came crashing through the trees.

'You must leave immediately, the hunters are here again. Go quickly and I'll meet up with you later. But be careful!' And off he went.

'Don't leave me here alone,' cried Dog. 'I don't want to go back to the men with guns.'

'You can come along with us then,' said Mother. 'You might be useful.'

So, Grumpus, Mother and Dog made their way quickly down to the large lake again.

They crossed the shallow water to the other side, then walked through woodlands until they reached the river.

'This part of the river is deep, so we must swim to the other side,' said Mother,

'Can you swim Dog?'

'Yes, I can do the doggie paddle.'

'Good, and you know how to swim, Grumpus, don't you?'

'Well, yes. Father taught me, but I'm not very good,' he said worriedly.'

'Well, it's not far, you'll be fine, and I'll help you. Just remember to paddle your legs and keep your mouth closed. Okay, let's go.'

All three jumped into the swirling river and swam as quickly as they could to the opposite bank. Mother climbed out, grabbed Grumpus and put him up on the grass, then picked up Dog and put him next to her son.

That was scary, thought Grumpus,

They shook themselves dry and began the long climb up the mountainside. It was getting dark and the two youngsters were tired, but hearing more gun shots in the distance they travelled on until they reached a small cave hidden in the rock face behind some very big bramble bushes.

'We can wait here and rest until the morning, because tomorrow we will move on to our new home on the other side of the mountain,' said Mother.

But neither dog nor Grumpus heard a word as they were fast asleep curled up cosily on piles of leaves in the safety of the den.

THE HUNTERS

Early next morning Dog was growling very quietly, but loud enough to wake Grumpus.

'What's the matter?' he asked sleepily.

'Shush, I heard voices.'

'Where's Mother?'

'I don't know.'

They both went to the den's entrance and crouched down behind the bushes to look outside.

They could see four men walking quickly down the hill with large guns slung over their shoulders.

Suddenly, one man stopped, looked over to the bramble bush in front of the cave, and started to walk towards it. Closer, closer and closer, he came.

Grumpus could hardly breathe he was so frightened.

'Well, what have we here?'

Grumpus thought his own heartbeat would give him away it was so loud, but just as the man bent down, brave little Dog flew at him and bit his nose as hard as he could.

'Ouch, that hurt! Hey boys, guess what? I've found Joe's little dog, the one that ran away yesterday. At first I thought it was one of those bear cubs we saw the other day.'

But his companions had already gone down the hill and didn't hear him.

'Will you stop biting me and wriggling so much. I'll have to leave you here until I find your master. He delved down into his bag and found a piece of string which he put around Dog's neck and tied him to a young tree trunk then off he went to find his friends.

Grumpus waited for a few minutes until the coast was clear, then went running up to Dog.

'Oh, thank you for saving me. I was so frightened, and you were so brave, but we must get you out of here.'

Although Grumpus was a young bear, he was quite strong, and he pushed and pulled with all his might to break the small tree to free his new friend. After what seemed a very long time, the young sapling snapped with a soft cracking sound. Dog was free, although he still had a piece of string around his neck with a trailing lead, but that didn't matter.

'I wonder where Mother is? I hope she comes back soon, because we can't stay out in the open too long. We must hide.

I know, I can climb that fir tree and hide amongst the branches. That's easy, and I think you're small enough to hide down that fox hole. The men won't see you if I cover the entrance with some leaves.'

Dog squeezed into the small space and Grumpus gathered up some dry leaves and put them in front of the hole, then he just managed to climb up to one of the lower branches when he heard the hunters coming back.

'He's gone. Your dog was here, I tied him up to that sapling that's now on the ground,' said the man with the swollen red nose.'

'Well, he's not here now,' said Joe, looking all about. 'I wonder where he is?'

The four men searched and searched calling and whistling for Dog, but finally gave up when there was no sign of him. 'Perhaps we'll find him tomorrow,' said Joe despondently, and they all walked back down the hill, leaving Dog and Grumpus in their hiding places.

As soon as they had gone out of sight Mother appeared from behind some trees from where she had been waiting. Grumpus saw her and scrambled down the tree in seconds.

'Mother, where have you been?'

'I went to the river to get some fish, but

then I saw the hunters and came back. But tell me what happened here?'

Grumpus told his mother everything whilst he scraped the leaves away from the fox hole to let Dog out.

'You did very well, I am very proud of both of you, but now we must travel further up the mountain where it will be safe.'

'When are we going to have breakfast? I'm hungry.'

'Well, we cannot stop now, but there will be plenty of acorns, roots, nuts and berries on our way and I will catch some fish as soon as I can.'

I don't eat nuts and berries, but I like fish, thought Dog, *perhaps I will try a worm or two!*

DYLAN

'I hope my friends are alright,' said Grumpus. 'I was with them when we heard the first gunshots.'

'Don't worry. I saw them earlier,' said Mother, 'and they're travelling a different route. I'm sure they'll be fine and you'll see them soon.' They all set off again, it was a lovely morning, the sun was shining and there was a soft breeze. Dog was sniffing the air and listening intently, which allowed the bears to relax and enjoy the walk as they climbed up and around the mountain.

But then, Dog looked up and became very excited.

Mother stopped. 'Is someone coming?'

'Yes, yes,' Dog said excitedly, 'but don't worry, it's Dylan, my first master's son, and my own mother, Old Dog.'

The bears stood completely still, but Dog yapped and pranced around until his mother, a much larger version of her son, came running up to him, her tail wagging with joy at seeing her Little Dog again.

Then Dylan came through the bushes and couldn't believe his eyes as his Old Dog and Little Dog were playing with a bear cub with a grumpy face, while an enormous brown grizzly bear looked on.

'I have missed you so much,' said Dylan, picking up Little Dog.

Grumpus watched carefully, and was so surprised when Dylan bent down and tickled his ears. *This is great*, he thought, then rolled over hoping that the boy would tickle his tummy. Which, to his delight, he did just that.

Mother, watched from under the trees as Grumpus, Old Dog, Little Dog and Dylan all played together in the grass.

'We had better go now,' said Dylan, after some time. 'We are staying nearby for the holidays and lunch will be ready, and everybody will be so pleased to see you

again Little Dog. We all really missed you. My father won't sell you again.'

Little Dog said goodbye to Grumpus and thanked Mother for her kindness. He said he hoped that they would all meet up again soon.

'Not all men and dogs are horrible, are they, Mother?' asked Grumpus.

'No, son, but you can never be sure, so you must always be very careful when you meet people and animals that you don't know.'

The two bears walked for a long time until they found the cave that would be their new home. It was very deep, and the entrance was well hidden by big bushes. Down below they could see another part of the river glinting in the evening sunshine.

'This is lovely,' cried Grumpus, 'it's better than where we used to live. I do hope Spike and Ted won't live too far away so we can explore together.'

THE PICNIC

'Where am I?' It was so very dark in the cave that Grumpus couldn't see anything. As he listened he couldn't hear anything either. Then he heard a thumping noise, but it was only his heart beating very loudly and very fast. He laid in the silent darkness and tried to think where he was.

Oh, now I remember. I am in my new home.

He cautiously stood up and could see a pinprick of light shining through at one end of the cave, so he walked slowly towards it and soon he was at the entrance. He peeked outside and saw a brilliant blue sky with the morning sun shining through the tall fir trees. He sniffed the cool clean air of the mountainside.

Oh this is lovely, he thought to himself.

He looked around, but he was alone, so he shook himself rigorously to dislodge the earth and leaves that had clung to his shiny brown fur and set off to explore his new territory and hopefully to find some breakfast, because as usual, he was very hungry.

He walked happily down the mountain whilst carefully picking his way through some prickly bushes until he saw a sandy path with big trees looming on either side.

This will lead down to the river and Mother might be there catching some fish, he thought.

He went down a little further until he could just see the water, then froze with fright. He could hear human voices.

Oh no! Not the hunters again. I must hide.

He looked up and knew a tree would be the best place again, so he scrambled up the nearest one as quickly as he could and sat trembling on a high branch.

Two boys and two girls came into view as he peered down through the foliage. They were laughing and talking and happily kicking a large blue and white football. They didn't see the little bear cub up in the tree as they went on downhill towards the river.

When they had gone, and all was quiet,

Grumpus climbed down and went to see where the children had gone. The boys were in the river splashing about and the girls were swimming up and down near the bank.

Mother wasn't there so breakfast would have to wait!

Eventually, when the children had had enough of the water they came back and sat on the grassy river bank, opened their rucksacks and took out all sorts of food. Grumpus could see sandwiches and apples and biscuits and cake. His mouth watered, and his tummy grumbled with hunger, but he couldn't get near the river without being seen, so he still had to wait.

After eating some of their picnic the children sat for awhile chatting and laughing, and then they played some more football until they all went for a walk and left the rest of the food by their rucksacks.

Grumpus waited for a few minutes until he couldn't hear their voices. When it was quiet he went very quickly over to where the children had been sitting, settled himself down on the grass and ate a whole tuna fish sandwich, four chocolate bars, one slice of honey cake two apples and two pears.

After he had eaten everything he could find, he went for a splash about in the cool river water. But he soon became bored on his own and decided to try and catch a fish, but he couldn't see any, so he waded in deeper and deeper until all too quickly the current became so strong it whisked him off his feet and carried him rapidly downstream. His legs were paddling hard but he couldn't swim against the fast flow of the river and he was being taken further and further downstream, his head bobbed in and out of the water, he opened his mouth and water rushed in, he couldn't breathe, and he was panicking. Then, suddenly, he was being lifted out of the water by a strong pair of hands.

'Little bear, what are you doing in the water? It's very dangerous to swim here when you are so small.'

Grumpus opened his eyes to see Dylan and Dog. 'Oh! Hello Dog,' he cried breathlessly.

'You are lucky we are staying in a log cabin nearby for the holidays, but you might not be so lucky next time, so don't go in this river by yourself until you are older,' scolded Dylan. 'You can fish and paddle in safety in lots of the small streams further up the mountain.'

'Thank you,' whispered Grumpus meekly. 'I'll look for them tomorrow.'

Dog pranced around and tried to lick Grumpus dry, he was so pleased to see him.

'Stop it Dog, you are making me wetter,' giggled Grumpus. However, they soon had to say their goodbyes as Dylan was in a hurry to get back to his friends and his picnic.

I hope I didn't eat Dylan's sandwiches, thought Grumpus guiltily.

He returned home feeling quite lonely. He did miss Spike and Ted and Dog. He wished he had a brother or sister. But he was very tired and as his mother wasn't back yet he went right to the back of the cave where it was dark and settled down for an afternoon nap.

'Grumpus, wake up. There's a surprise for you out here,' called Mother.

Grumpus shook himself, and went sleepily to the cave entrance. He couldn't see a surprise. There was no one there, not even his mother, and it was all very quiet. He was just going back to finish his sleep, thinking he must have been dreaming, when from behind a bush out jumped Spike and Ted. They were all so excited. They rolled over and over, arms and legs all tangled up, all three of them squealing with delight.

'What a lovely surprise!'

'Let's meet up here tomorrow so we can show you our new den, we don't live far away,' said Spike.

'Oh yes, then we can go exploring and have lots more new adventures together,' said Grumpus very happily.

DID YOU KNOW?

1. Brown bears love roots, and berries and fish, but will also eat all sorts of food when they are hungry – including your picnic.

2. When brown grizzly bears are fully grown, they are too big to climb trees.

3. Salmon are the favourite fish for brown bears.

4. Brown bears are very good swimmers.

5. When brown bears are fully grown, they can go without food during hibernation for five or six months in the winter.

6. North American brown bears like Grumpus are called Grizzly Bears.